# Spudboy and Chip

## By

## David Windle

Cover illustration: Gavin Dobson

Cover design: Emma Smith

ISBN-13: 978-1543147025
ISBN-10: 154314702X

# Chapter 1

## Potato Volcano

"Come on, Colin, eat up. You won't grow
big and strong unless you do," Dad said,
pushing my plate right under my nose. "Sticky
Toffee Trifle flavour mashed potato. This one's
a winner!"

There was no way I could force down
another mouthful. I'd reached my potato limit; I
was at maximum mash! I'd already eaten a
whole plate of Bacon and Avocado mash, and
that was on top of a giant pile of Chilli and
Cheese flavour.

"Susan, this is your best yet. It's the perfect potato pudding. If this doesn't sell like hot cakes in Mama Sludge's, nothing will!"

Dad looked down at the kitchen floor as he spoke, as if he was trying to imagine all the customers in Mama Sludge's, our fish and chip shop, which was below the flat. We used to have tonnes of customers at Mama Sludge's because Mum made the best chips in all of London. Maybe in all of the UK? Maybe in all the World? Maybe in the whole Univ...you get the picture.

"Colin? What about you? Does it taste like a hot cake to you?"

I stared at the glistening heap in front of me and blinked. I was seriously sick of mashed potato. The trouble was, Mama Sludge's was in danger of closing down for good! Ever since the High Street had filled up with cafes and restaurants like Pizzarama and Brillo-Burger, we'd had hardly any customers, so Mum had decided we needed to try something new.

"As I always tell my customers: fish is just a side dish, the potato's the main meal," Mum said, "and I haven't slaved over a hot masher for you to turn your nose up, have I My Little Peeler?

Mum always called me Her Little Peeler because I peeled the potatoes every night and took the peelings down to the basement bins.

"Your sister always ate her spuds, and look at her now. If you want to get anywhere in life you need to shovel it down, my boy," Dad told me.

"We're so proud of Kerry, aren't we, Terry?" cooed Mum.

"We certainly are, Sue," said Dad, giving, Mum's hand a squeeze. "Your brother ate his tatties too and we all know how well he's doing these days," Dad went on, his mash speckled moustache bobbling as he spoke.

Ever since my brainiac sister Kerry had gone off to university to become even brainier and my 'Captain of Every School Team' brother, Murray, had won a scholarship to a special sports academy, it'd just been Mum, Dad and me.

I blinked behind my glasses. I wasn't doing brilliantly at anything at school; not at maths, not at English, definitely not at sport, and I was the worst artist in the universe, I couldn't even draw a realistic stick man. I know stick men aren't meant to look like real people,

but I couldn't even draw one that looked like a

stick man.

"The thing about the potato," Dad began,

tapping the table top with his knuckles, "is that

it's full of pure health..."

"As long as you don't fry it to death," said

Mum.

"...It's got more vitamin C in it than a

tomato," said Dad, giving the table another tap.

"...and more potassium than a banana,"

Mum said, smiling.

"…and enough iron in it to make a suit of armour!" Dad cheered, pointing his knife like a sword.

I'd heard all these potato health facts a million times before. I had no idea what potassium was but vitamin C was a vitamin so it *had* to be good for you. I'd never seen a suit of armour made of potato, though.

"And," said Dad, raising a finger to the ceiling, "it's a carbohydrate, so it's packed with energy. These new flavours are going to transform our fortunes, Susan, I'm absolutely certain of it."

I looked at the mash mountain on my plate. I couldn't have *climbed* it, let alone eaten it! Maybe my parents were right though? If I ate it all up, perhaps things would change for the better? Perhaps *I*'d change for the better!

Taking a deep breath, I lifted a fork full of Sticky Toffee Trifle mash to my mouth. My lips twitched; my tongue shivered. Sweat trickled down my forehead as the smell wafted up my nostrils. It was odd; it was wrong – a potato shouldn't smell of toffee! I gripped the fork and forced it towards my mouth.

RUMBLE

SQUIRGLE

GURGLE

Uh oh!

The mound of mash I'd already eaten was crammed in so tightly it could erupt at any moment. My eyelids started to flutter, my ears lobes blazed red hot. Dropping my fork onto my plate, I clamped my hand over my mouth.

"Colin, what's happening?" Dad murmured, his forehead crinkling.

I had to escape.

RUMBLE

BURPLE

KWERGLE

The potato volcano in my tummy leapt

into life. I had to get to the toilet before it was

too late. The trouble was, it was already too late.

As I turned to run, I tripped on the leg of my

chair and staggered into the kitchen table.

"Ooooff."

"Oh, My Little Peeler!"

"Euuuuurrggh!" I crumpled to the floor.

The red pattern on the kitchen lino swirled into

my eyes and round and round inside my head

like a bubbling cauldron of hot pink mashed

potato. As I rolled onto my back, my mouth

yawned open really wide.

"No, no!" cried Mum, "Quick, Terry get a bucket!"

BLAAAARGH!

The volcano in my tummy erupted and a jet of multi-coloured, multi-flavoured potato paste shot out straight into the air, before splattering down right on top of Dad's shiny, bald head.

"Oh Terry, Terry! Maybe toffee trifle isn't such a good idea after all?"

Dad quivered as potato puke dripped off his nose and onto the carpet. I blinked and blinked, but it didn't help.

"Colin, I think you should *probably* go upstairs to your room for a bit, OK?" he said at a last, his mouth hardly moving at all.

"OK," I said, and I was sick all over again.

# Chapter 2

## Spud Swamp

With my tummy still squirgling, I sat on the edge of my bed and looked around my room, which didn't take long because it was tiny. Even though Kerry and Murray had moved out, they came back during the holidays, so I couldn't move into one of their rooms. My room was the highest in the flat, because it used to be an attic, so I had to go up another tiny flight of stairs to get to it. From the window, I could see all the way down our road to the park at one

end and the high street at the other.

On the window sill, the red numbers on

my alarm clock said 7:00pm. Slumping onto my

bed, I blinked hard five times and put a hand on

my tummy, which was sticking out like a lump

of rock. My head felt mushy from all the potato

puking I'd done. There was a quiet knock and

my door opened a crack.

"Colin, it's me." Mum peeped in. "Are you

OK, My Little Peeler?"

"Think so," I said, sitting up slowly.

"Here." Mum handed me a glass of water

and I took a glug. "Dad's changing his shirt."

"Oh."

"And his trousers."

"Right."

"And his shoes and socks."

"Sorry."

"Why don't you take the peelings down to the bins for him? That'd cheer him up. Then you can come in and watch some TV with us, if you like."

Mum leant forward and kissed the top of my head. "Honestly, when will you learn not to eat so much mash, you've eaten yourself silly this time."

"But..."

"It's alright. It makes me happy knowing how much you love it. I'll leave the bag out in the kitchen."

With a belly like a boulder, I put on my trainers and struggled down to the kitchen.

The bin bag was stuffed full of rubbish, including at least a week's worth of potato peelings, which in the Sludge household was a lot of spud. It smelled worse than a cow's bum and a stream of brown juice trickled out of a hole in the bottom.

Closing my mouth tightly, I wrapped both my arms around the greasy black bag and hugged it. GROSS. It was like cuddling a massive ball of dung and I was a human dung beetle.

I waddled past the living room where Mum and Dad were watching TV, then down all twenty nine steps until, at last, I arrived at the basement. I turned and shoved the door open with my back, dragging the bag behind me. Inside, the air was cold and damp; like being in big fridge, only darker because the light bulb had broken months ago. Shivering, I dumped the bin liner on to the ground next to one of the wheelie bins.

"Yuck!"

A disgusting streak of gungy, brown week-old potato juice had smeared its way down my shirt.

"Double yuck..."

It was slowly seeping through the top of my trousers and into my pants.

"Oh....TRIPLE YUCK!"

Wrapping my arms round the bin bag again, I wriggled it up my body as high as I could. My eyes were watering with the stink but all I needed to do was jump a few centimetres and the bag would be in the bin. Job done. Then I could get out of the creepy basement.

"Come on, come on, you can do this, you can do this…" I told myself.  I took a step closer to the bin.

Uh-oh.

My foot landed right in a slippery puddle of sludge and skidded out from under me.

"AAAAAAAAAAAAARRRRGH!"

Clonk! I hit the floor hard and everything went black.

When I opened my eyes, I was lying on my back on the cold concrete. I tried to sit up, but something heavy was pinning me down and my skin was tingling all over. I was fizzing from head to foot!

"What the...?"

Glancing down, I saw a huge compost heap of potato peelings pressing me into the floor. Potato juice was soaking though my clothes and there was something wriggling, something alive, sitting in the middle of the heap.

"YUUUUUUUUUCK!"

I scrabbled to my feet, scattering potato bits everywhere. With the back of my head throbbing where I'd bashed it, my body buzzed like I'd been plugged into an electric socket. The tickly, tingly feeling grew stronger and stronger and stronger until I was shaking so much I thought my teeth were going to fall out. Then, it

stopped, leaving nothing but a puff of potatoey

steam in the air over my head.

# Chapter 3

## Serious Strangeness

*That was seriously strange.* I kicked a

gungy ball of potato peelings off my trainer. The

ball looped into the air, bounced off the wall

and landed in the wheelie bin.

*Wow*. Normally, I was rubbish at football.

"Woah! That was cooool. What are we

gonna do now?" said a voice.

I froze. A voice? In the basement?

There was no one else there, I was sure

of it. I hadn't seen anyone. In fact, I'd *never*

seen anyone else down in the basement in my

whole life. As far as I could tell, I was the only person who went down there.

"Hello?" I squeaked.

"Hi."

Spinning round, I peered back into the gloom through my specs.

"Hello?"

"Yeah, yeah you just said that. So, what's the plan, big guy?"

First left, then right, I stared into the shadows. There was no one there.

"Wh-where are you?"

"Where am I? I'm down here, big fella, right where you dropped me."

*Someone must've been trapped in the*

*rubbish bag!*

"DOWN HERE," the voice shouted.

I looked at the floor just in front of me,

and there, on a mound of peelings was a small,

slightly mouldy potato. And it was shouting. At

me.

I stared. And stared, and stared some

more.

"Hey, it's rude to stare, buddy," said the

potato.

"ARRRRRRRRRRRRGH!"

I sprinted back up all the steps. Without

slowing down, I hurtled up the final staircase to

the top floor, crashed into my bedroom and dived under my quilt, pulling it around me for extra-protection. Something very funny was going on. Normally, after running up three flights I couldn't breathe properly, but I wasn't out of breath at all. And, I'd just met a talking potato, hadn't I? *Weird.*

I blinked and blinked and blinked. It didn't help.

Then I remembered I was still wearing my filthy potato caked clothes and they'd be covering my bed in grossness.

As quickly as I'd leapt into bed, I sprang out and kicked my stained trainers into the far corner of my room...which wasn't very far away.

I peeled off my soggy shirt and trousers,

screwed them into a ball and lobbed them onto

the top of my wardrobe, where Mum wouldn't

find them. My pants and socks were soaked too

but before I could whip them off, I glimpsed my

reflection in the window.

For the second time that night, I froze.

My body looked wrong. Usually, my skin was as

pale as paper, but reflected in the black glass I

looked almost yellow. Not only that, but there

were horrible lumps, nobbles and dents

bursting out all over me and disgusting stringy

hairs sprouting from my shoulders.

Looking down, I gasped. Normally, my legs were two skinny twigs sticking out of my pants, but they'd transformed into hairy stumps, and my feet seemed to have grown extra toes which stuck out at all angles.

"No...no...no..." I whimpered, "It's not real. It's not real. It's not real."

It couldn't be. And neither could the talking potato. Potatoes don't talk. They are silent. Like carrots, or parsnips, or corn-on-the-cob.

After scrambling into my pyjamas, I drew the curtains so I couldn't see myself in the window, switched off the light and dived back under my quilt.

Running my fingers round the back of my head, I felt the large bump where I'd banged it on the concrete. That was it! I'd had a bang on the head and wasn't thinking straight. All I needed was some sleep and everything would be fine. When I woke up, everything would be back to normal, wouldn't it?

# Chapter 4

## Alarm Chip

Beep, beep, beep!

*Arrrgh, the alarm.*

Without opening my eyes, I reached over and pressed the off button.

Beep, beep, beep!

I pressed it again, harder this time. The clock was a hand-me-down from Murray and the button didn't always work straight away.

Beep, beep, beep!

"Stupid alarm clock." I smashed my fist onto the button. That normally stopped it.

"Hey, don't take it out on the alarm clock, dude!"

The voice. It was back, and in my room.

"I'm the one you should be hitting. Listen – beep, beep, beep. It's me that woke you up."

I grabbed my glasses from down the side of my bed and hooked them over my ears. The clock said 4:48am and outside the sun was just beginning to rise, giving my room an orange glow.

"You shouldn't leave your window open. Makes it very easy for burglars, you know."

The mouldy potato was sitting on the window sill, next to Murray's alarm clock.

"But we're on the 3rd floor," I heard myself say, without really believing I was saying it.

"Yeah, but I can jump very high, when I put my mind to it."

"Can you? But you're...a potato..."

"Well spotted, big guy. Nothing gets past you does it?"

The creature on the ledge seemed to be looking at me, although it didn't have a face exactly, just a few marks and patches which where a face might be, if potatoes had faces. My mouth opened and closed, but no words came out.

"Yeah, I know I'm not looking my best. I've got a bit of mould going on and someone's taken a slice out of my behind. Look."

The potato span round on its end and showed me a circle of white potato flesh with no peel on it, exactly where a behind would be if potatoes had behinds.

"But, like I said earlier, it's rude to stare."

"This isn't real, this isn't real," I murmured.

"It's real, my friend," said the potato, rolling off the window ledge and landing in the middle of my bed, where it leant against a ripple in the quilt, "they call me Chip. Pleased to meet you."

I gawped.

"I'd shake your hand but I haven't got a hand to shake with." Chip chuckled, his little potato body jiggling up and down. "So, what's your name, buddy?"

My mouth moved, but nothing came out again.

"Quiet one, aren't you?"

"Colin Sludge," I said, robotically.

"Sludge? Oooh that is *unlucky,* dude," said the potato, "you should get that changed."

"Changed?"

"Yeah, you know to something snappy like, Colin Potatoford...no that's no good... How about Colin Muddenspud?"

The potato looked up at me. I looked back at him.

"Nah, you're right, we need to lose the Colin," he said, "Let's keep it simple: Spudman? No, that's no good....ah ha...I've got it...Spudboy. It's got a ring to it hasn't it? Spudboy – half boy, half potato! There we go. Perfect."

The potato lay down on its side and rolled up the bed until it was right under my nose.

"Do you have any idea what is going on?" it asked, perching on the edge of the quilt.

I shook my head.

"Well, let me tell you, I've been waiting for this moment all my life. It gets pretty dull trying to make conversation with potatoes all the time. Most of them are idiots."

I pulled the quilt up higher as the potato leant towards me.

"But there's something about you which makes you the perfect balance of person and potato. Just like me."

"I'm nothing like you," I croaked.

"Oh yes you are."

"Oh no I'm not."

"You are."

"I'm not."

"Are."

"Not."

The potato smiled, or at least the little scratch it seemed to be using for a mouth curled up at the ends.

"We'll see," it said and it rolled off the bed, onto the carpet and under the wardrobe.

"Time for a snooze, I think."

"This isn't real, this isn't real," I

murmured again, rubbing the bump on the back

of my head, which felt as big as a brick.

# Chapter 5

## Potato Chucker

Beep beep beep!

*Arrgh, the alarm.*

I hadn't slept very well.

Blinking to clear my head, I found my glasses down the side of my bed and hooked them over my ears. Keeping as much of myself under the quilt as I could, I scanned the carpet. There was no sign of the talking potato. I must've imagined it. It was the only explanation.

I felt for the bump on the back of my head with my fingers. It was still there, but a lot smaller, more like a pebble than a brick.

Shivering, I remembered my strange yellow body, swollen feet and hairy shoulders from the night before and hoped more than anything I'd imagined that too. I lifted the quilt to take a look. Poking out of the end of my pyjama bottoms, my feet looked totally normal.

Phew.

I *had* imagined it.

Flinging back the duvet, I rolled out of bed and onto the floor. I needed to check under the wardrobe to make sure there were no talking vegetables.

There wasn't a potato in sight.

Brilliant!

I jumped up. 7.45am – that only gave me half an hour to get ready, before I had to leave for school. It was going to be tight!

Exactly twenty-four minutes later I was standing on the pavement, with my school bag over my shoulder, looking back up at my bedroom window. I'd never got ready so quickly in my life. For someone who'd hardly slept, I was feeling pretty springy.

Since being in Year 5, I'd walked to school on my own, which was a good thing as Mum and Dad were often tired from working late at Mama Sludge's.

After walking for a few minutes, I stopped. Something felt wrong. The hairs on the back of my neck were tingling like antennae. I was being watched. I knew it. Turning round slowly, I looked back down the street. Funny. There was no one there. All I could see was the little park at the end and rows of terraced houses down either side of it.

I carried on walking but the creepy feeling wouldn't go away so I stopped again and looked around. Nope. No one. Just me and a few fat looking pigeons.

"Hey Spudboy, are you homesick or something? If we keep stopping to look at your flat, we're gonna be late for school."

My stomach nearly somersaulted right out of my mouth.

The voice. The potato! "Arrgh!"

"OK. Keep calm, big guy. I'm in here."

My school bag shook. I was going mad. This couldn't be happening. I chucked the bag on to the grass by the road.

"Hey, take it easy. It's cramped in here!" the voice called up through a hole by the strap.

"It's not real, it's not real." My blinking had gone into overdrive. I glared at my bag. It was haunted! I wanted to squash it, crush it, bin it.

"Morning, Colin. Everything OK there, young man?"

It was Mrs Sticklebee, who lived next door but one. Flattening my hair with my hand, I tried to look as normal as possible.

"Yes, fine thank you."

"Oh good. It's just you're shouting at your school bag." She pointed her walking stick at my bag.

"I know...er...forgot my homework. I've got to walk all the way home again to get it."

Her fuzzy little dog, Milton, was sizing up

my bag for a wee.

"Well, Colin, it's not your bag's fault is it?"

She smiled and I could see a gap where one of

her front teeth was missing.

"No, it's not."

"Milton! Leave that bag alone you rascal!"

she snapped. "Have a good day, Colin."

Mrs Sticklebee and Milton trundled off in

the direction of the shops. I waited until they

were out of sight before picking my bag up and

gripping it hard.

"Phew! That was close. That mutt almost gave me a soaking," came the voice from inside again.

"I'm not listening to you," I said, unzipping the bag and tipping it up so everything fell out onto the pavement. Two pencils, one trainer, a pair of shorts, a reading book, loads of crumbs from a cookie and one manky old potato.

"Gotcha!" I said, clutching the spud in my fingers. Then I took a run up and threw it as far as I could. "Wow!"

Usually, my throwing was rubbish but it

flew through the air like a missile and vanished

into a patch of bushes by some bins.

I bet even Murray would've been

impressed by that.

# Chapter 6

## Robo-Wasp Attack

As soon as I arrived at school I spotted danger.

Spike Blagger was leaning against the wall by the school gate with his hands in his pockets and a lot of gel in his hair. Darius Gizmo was fiddling with his mobile phone; Darius was always fiddling with his phone.

"Look who it is, Darius," Spike sneered as I walked up, "Sludgy, sludgy sluuuuuuuuudge."

Darius looked up from his phone and grinned. I blinked a few times and tried to tuck my head down between my shoulders. Spike stepped out and blocked my way.

"Blink, blink, blinketty blink," he said, doing big blinks right up close to my face. "Blink and you'll miss it."

"What?" I blinked. I couldn't help it.

"This!"

"Owwwww!" I yelped as something bit my nose.

"HA HA HA!" Spike and Darius exploded with laughter.

"What was that?" My nose throbbed.

"Tell him, Darius."

Darius Gizmo waved his phone in the air.

"My latest invention," he said, still grinning. He was always grinning. A large fly with a black and yellow back landed on his shoulder. "I call it Robo-wasp. I made it at home out of my dad's old laptop."

As he pressed the screen on his mobile phone, the metal fly's wings flapped up and down.

"I reckon I can work out how to control anything from my phone."

Darius was a bit of a genius. His mum was a scientist, who worked for the government on top secret projects, and she must've handed her brains down to her son. The only thing my mum handed to me was a potato peeler.

Gizmo's inventions were always trouble. Last week, he'd invented an automatic bum pincher and the week before that he'd hacked into the school's computer records and given Spike top marks in everything. Darius already had top marks in everything.

In class, Spike and Darius sat at the back as usual. I was a few tables in front of them. From their chuckles I could tell they were up to something.

As soon as Ms Brimstone starting calling the register, I heard it. A faint buzz. I turned and looked at Darius, who was hiding his hand under his desk. I ducked and peeked under and, just as I thought, he had his mobile phone out, controlling Robo-wasp. Mobile phones were against school rules and so were robot wasps.

"Colin Sludge, sit up and look this way," Ms Brimstone boomed.

"But Darius has..."

"We are silent during register, Colin." She put her pink finger up to her lips and stared at me over her glasses. Ms Brimstone always wore a pink flowery shirt and a blue skirt. Her hair was grey and often in a pile on her head. I think she was at least 40.

She went back to calling the register.

Bzzzzzzz, Robo-wasp buzzed a metre above everyone's heads. It zoomed past me, its sharp metal sting poking out of the end of its body like a pin. Its legs looked like they were made out of folded out paper clips.

"Darius Gizmo."

"Here, Ms Brimstone," Darius replied, sounding like the most sensible person in the world. Darius was very good at pretending to be good.

My nose still hurt from where it had been stung. The wasp moved over each person in turn, hovering above their head, choosing its next victim. Or rather Darius and Spike were choosing *their* next victim.

I had to do something. But if I said anything, then Darius and Spike would be after revenge and wouldn't stop until they got it.

Robo-wasp landed on Alfie Radish's head. He was sitting three seats in front of me. The wasp was balanced right on the edge of his hair, just above his ear. He hadn't noticed. I shifted my bum from side to side. My feet started to tap and I blinked. I had to say something. But I couldn't. I opened my mouth but nothing came out.

"Tabitha Lightwell."

"Yes, Ms Brimstone."

"Toby Ornotoby."

"Yes, Ms Brimstone."

"Alfie Radish."

"Yes, Ms Brimstone."

I squeezed my eyes shut really tightly then opened them as wide as I could, like a signal to Alfie. It didn't help. My heart was beating so hard I thought my eyes were going to pop out.

"Eddie Zedder."

"Yes, Ms Brimstone."

Robo-wasp had crawled down the side of Alfie's head and was sitting on top of his ear. He still hadn't noticed! Behind me, Spike and Darius were whispering.

Anger swept through me making my face burn and my shoulders itch.  In an instant, my shirt was soaked with sweat. And so were my trousers and socks. I was leaking from everywhere.

My body felt like it was being turned inside out!

Horrified, I looked down at my fingers...they were going bumpy and knobbly, like bits of tree stump. As liquid started to drip out of the ends of my shirt sleeves, I knew I had to get out of there! I had to escape.

"Ms Brimstone."

"Colin?"

"I have to go to the..."

"Toilet?"

"Yes!" I raced for the class room door.

"Euurgh, he's all greasy!" screamed

Tabitha as I dashed by.

"Gross!" shrieked Sarah.

As I stumbled out into the hallway, I

could hear the whole class laughing.

"Silence!" Ms Brimstone roared, but the

laughing carried on.

I ran to the boys' toilets and threw myself

into a cubicle, locking the door behind me.

*What was going on?*

# Chapter 7

## The Return of the Chip

My shoulders burnt and tingled as if they were crawling with red ants. I ran my fingers inside my shirt collar and felt the bottom of my neck.

No! No! This couldn't be happening!

Long strands of thin hair were popping up and out of my skin. Little lumps and bumps were bursting out of me everywhere. My head felt fuzzy and light so I sat down on the toilet seat. Crack! The force of my bum on the plastic seat snapped it off the toilet completely. My insides rippled. I was going to be sick *again*. I jammed my hands against the walls to steady myself and the whole toilet cubicle rattled and wobbled as if it was in an earthquake. Everything I touched nearly broke!

My skin was getting harder and harder like a shell.

Oh no! No!

I scrunched my eyes closed completely and kept them that way. Whatever was happening to me, I didn't want to see it.

"Hey! Hey!"

The voice.

I kept my eyes shut. I was imagining it. It was all part of this crazy trick someone was playing on me.

"Yo! I said, YO!"

Something bashed against my foot.

"YO!"

I opened my eyes.

"Hey, dude. It's me – Chip – your long lost potato pal."

"Hello," I said, shakily.

"Thanks for giving me the old heave-ho back there. But you won't get rid of me that easily. I can roll like the wind."

"You rolled here?"

"All the way. I saw what those boys did to you at the gate too."

"Oh."

"Not good, dude."

"No. I suppose not. How did you get in here?"

"I just rolled right through the front door. No one said a word to me. Then I saw you running about like a fool so I followed you in here. Easy."

The potato hopped up onto the end of my shoe and bounced up and down twice like a tennis ball.

BOING!

The third time it bounced it landed on my

lap, and looked at me with its strange scratchy

face.

"How're ya feeling now, kiddo? You

looked pretty ropey a moment ago."

I hadn't even noticed, but I'd stopped

sweating. The skin on my hands looked less

bumpy too.

"I think I'm OK."

"You *are* OK, big guy!"

"Am I?"

"Yeah," the potato said, curling up his

mouth scratch in a smile and raising what might

have been his eyebrows. "The merging process isn't easy."

"Merging?"

"Yeah. Your human cells are still joining together with the potato ones. Becoming potato powered isn't instant, you know. It takes a bit of time to settle in."

I blinked.

"You blink a lot, don't ya?"

I nodded and blinked again.

Knock, knock.

"Colin? Colin? Are you in there?"

It was Alfie Radish. I could see his polished black school shoes through the gap under the door.

"Quick, put me in your pocket," whispered Chip.

"Are you real?"

"I'm just as real as anyone else, Spudboy, my friend. Now put me in your pocket, and let's go."

"Are you on the phone, Colin? Phones are against school rules," Alfie said, his shoes shining.

"I'll be one second, Alfie."

I picked Chip up. He felt just like a potato. He looked just like a potato. The only difference was he talked.

"I think I've gone mad," I told him, and slipped him into my pocket. I looked at my hands; my skin had gone totally back to normal and there wasn't a single sign of sweatiness. I had to get home and ask Mum to take me to the doctor's. Not only was my body going bonkers, I was talking to a *potato*. Eating potatoes is one thing, but talking to them is something far worse. It must be a sign of serious illness. There's no way I'd ever be as clever as Kerry or as sporty as Murray with this happening to me.

If the doctor could give me some pills to make

me better, then I could just get on with trying

not to be rubbish at things like usual.

Unfortunately, Alfie Radish had other ideas.

"Ms Brimstone says we need to get our

packed lunches and meet everyone in the

playground. They're already queuing for the

coach," Alfie told me as we walked back down

the corridor.

"Where are we going?"

"It's the Science Museum trip, Colin!"

Oh yeah. I'd completely forgotten about

that. One of Alfie's ears was red and swollen.

"What happened to your ear, Alfie?" I

asked.

"I think a bee stung me. It really hurt."

# Chapter 8

## The Flight of Our Lives

After filling in our quizzes, doing some experiments with magnets and watching a show about electricity, we filed into the Science Museum's lunch room. Chip was still in my pocket. He hadn't said a word since we were in the toilet cubicle hours ago. Maybe I was imagining it after all? I hoped so.

"Move down the bench please, Tabitha," bellowed Ms Brimstone.

"I am not sitting next to him!"

She pointed at me.

"Tabitha, take your seat."

"I'm not sitting next to Colin. He's covered in grease. I might get it on my dress."

Everyone started sniggering. Spike Blagger and Darius Gizmo sat on the bench across the table from me. Darius got his phone out straight away.

"Don't worry Colin, I've left my pet Robo-Wasp back at school. Didn't want to risk losing him here."

"Oh! Oh! Ms Brimstone I need the....toilet!" jeered Spike, popping open his packed lunch and pulling out a sausage roll.

"Here you go, Colin," said Ms Brimstone, handing me a spare packed lunch. As I'd forgotten about the trip, I hadn't brought one.

"Sludgy sludgy sludge sludge..." Spike hissed at me, "I think I'm going to blink. Blink blink blink."

Darius giggled next to him, so did Sarah next to him, and Helen and Toby. Alfie Radish slid into the empty space next to me and without looking up at the laughing faces opposite, took a cheese sandwich out of his see-through plastic lunch box. His ear still looked red and it was sticking a long way out of the side of his head, as if it had been stretched.

"How's your lughole, Radish?" said Spike, smirking.

"OK thanks, Spike. I think it'll get better soon," Alfie replied, before taking a bite of his plain cheese sandwich.

Ms Brimstone stood at the end of the long dining table.

"After lunch, the Science Museum has a very special treat for us," she said, "and this gentleman will be our guide for the final part of our trip today."

Ms Brimstone stepped aside and behind her was a tall, skinny man in a bright green t-shirt and zig-zaggy hair.

"Hello, Year 5. Welcome!" He wafted his hand over his head and bowed like an actor. He bent so far over, the tips of his hair touched the floor. He bowed for ages. "My name is Fernando Faffernelli," he said, when he finally came up again, "and I will be your guide for our interactive Lunar Landing exhibition."

"Ooooooo!" everyone said.

"So eat up, and let's get into orbit!"

"Yeah!" Everyone cheered and began shovelling their packed lunches into their mouths extra-fast.

I finished my sandwich. Opposite, Darius was showing Spike something on his mobile.

"Yes!" Spike shouted and they gave each other a high five.

"Follow me Year 5," Fernando said, holding his hand in the air like a flag.

He led us back through all the exhibitions to the entrance hall.

"Here we are," he said, "I don't expect any of you noticed this door when you arrived earlier."

He stepped to the side. Behind him was a single white door.

"Not everyone gets to go in here. But, you're the lucky ones!"

Pulling a key from his trouser pocket, he turned and slid it into the lock.

"Outer space here we come!" he sang, and we all followed him into the secret room.

"Wow!" said Alfie Radish, next to me as we gathered round the enormous white rocket on a platform in the middle of the room. Over our heads the ceiling was made of glass, so you could see right out into the sky.

"Yes, WOW!" Fernando said, his hair as shiny as Alfie's shoes. "This is an *exact* replica of the space rocket that first took man to the moon. And, guess what..."

"What?" we all shouted.

"Today, it's your turn to take a ride in it."

"Wow!"

Darius Gizmo put up his hand.

"Yes, young man?"

"It can't be an exact replica, because the original rocket could never fit twenty eight school children on board, could it Mr Fattybelly?"

The crowd giggled.

"Shhhh children," said Ms Brimstone, giving us her most terrifying glare.

"Aha, no, you are right. It is not an exact replica. And my name is Faffernelli, not Fattybelly."

"Surely, it's a simulator? Real flight would be impossible from inside the Science Museum," Darius said.

A grimace flashed across Fernando's face, before he forced it into a smile.

"Well, you are a little clever clogs aren't you? You have a good point, young man. Today, you will be using it as a simulator. We aren't actually going to the moon. But you will experience what it is *like* to take off and land on the moon, which is just as good, only a lot safer for school children. Watch!"

Fernando danced up the steps to the platform, stretched out a long finger and pressed a button on the side of the rocket.

Schoooooop.

The rocket door slid open.

"In we go," he said with a wave, "prepare for the flight of your life!"

# Chapter 9

## Blast Off!

With Alfie Radish just behind me, I jogged

up the steps onto the platform.

"I'll sit next to you, Colin."

"Thanks, Alfie."

Inside, the walls of the rocket were made

of crinkled silver foil. There was a row of red

seats down each side of the aisle and a round

window by each seat.

"These chairs have been put in to the

rocket for the simulator. Sit down quickly and

do up your seat belt," Fernando said, "I'm just going to get changed."

He disappeared behind a thick velvety curtain at the front.

"I never knew they had curtains in space ships," Alfie said as we clipped our seatbelts around our waists.

"Me neither."

"Ta-dah!"

The curtain flew open and Fernando reappeared dressed in a real spaceman uniform. Behind him was a desk full of flashing buttons and screens, with a control stick in the middle.

And, like a massive car windscreen, the cockpit window looked out over the front of the rocket.

"If you reach under your seat, you'll find a space helmet of your own," he said.

Everyone began rummaging under their seats and putting their helmets on.

"This is brilliant!" said Alfie.

I felt a tingly tickle run down the back of my neck. Something was happening behind me. Looking over my shoulder, I noticed Spike and Darius talking to Ms Brimstone in the back seat.

Ms Brimstone stood up and strode down the aisle.

"Fernando, these two boys need to visit the toilet, can we let them go before take-off?" she asked.

Fernando frowned.

"Hmmm, I don't know. We are locking the cabin door in one minute. If they go now, they might miss the flight."

Ms Brimstone looked back at Spike and Darius. Spike pulled a face like he was desperate for a wee.

"I'm gonna burst, Miss," he whimpered.

Ms Brimstone sighed.

"OK, well, off you two go. If you're late for take-off, then you'll miss the trip."

"Thanks, Miss," Spike said, as he and Darius scurried back down the rocket and out the door. As he passed by me, I was sure Spike winked at Darius and they were both smiling. I felt a twitch in my tummy and someone was punching my leg from inside my pocket.

Chip had woken up at last.

Alfie tapped me on the shoulder and gave me a thumbs-up.

Inside his space helmet, his mouth moved but I couldn't hear a word he said. There was a little catch on the side of the helmet, I flicked it and the glass front flipped open.

"Put yours on, Colin, it's great!" Alfie panted. For some reason, I didn't want to put mine on. Something told me, it wasn't a good idea. My neck was still tingling and my shoulders were itching.

Just then Fernando skipped down the aisle. "Right. We need to lock the door and get going. I've got another group to take up after you. Are those boys back yet?"

"I'm afraid not," said Ms Brimstone.

"We have no choice but to leave without them," Fernando said dramatically, clunking the cabin door closed and twisting the lever to lock it.

Alfie bounced up and down next to me.

Across the aisle, Tabitha and Sarah were holding

hands and crossing their fingers.

Fernando raced back to the controls.

"Prepare for blast off, Year 5," he

announced, leaping into the pilot's seat. A large

green button flashed on the control panel.

Fernando pressed it.

ZZZZZZZZZZZZ

The rocket slowly started lifting up until

its nose pointed to the ceiling and we were all

hanging in the air facing upwards in our chairs.

"It's like a roller coaster," whispered Alfie.

An American voice came out of some speakers above our heads.

"Take off in 10…"

The whole class squealed.

"9."

My body began to sweat and my mouth dried out. In my pocket, Chip was going nuts. He was ramming his whole potatoey body into my leg.

"8."

Through the window next to my seat I could see Darius and Spike on the platform outside. Spike was hopping from foot to foot on the spot like a boxer, while Darius tapped the

screen on his mobile phone.

"7."

"Hey, Spudboy!"

"Chip."

The top of Chip's head or body, or

whatever it was, was poking out of my pocket.

"Does any of this feel right to you?"

"6."

"No."

"Me neither, kiddo."

"5."

The whole class joined in with the count down.

"4."

"3."

Electric shutters with pictures of stars and comets lowered over the windows, so we couldn't see out anymore, and the windscreen at the front flickered with images of outer space like a cinema.

"2."

"1."

"BLAST OFF!"

# Chapter 10

# Potato Power

As the jets roared, the tin foil walls vibrated. On the windscreen cinema we zoomed through the sky towards space.

"Wowee!" Alfie squeaked right next to me.

The rocket started to shake even more as we flew further and further from Earth.

"There might be a bit of turbulence as we leave the Earth's atmosphere," Fernando shouted over the noise.

Tabitha screamed.

"Keep calm Space Explorers!" Fernando sang. "Look, we're nearly out of the atmosphere."

On the screen the line between the blue sky and outer space was getting closer and closer as we raced along. The rocket shook and shook. The shutters rattled.

"Weeeeee! We're nearly in space, Colin," said Alfie.

BOOM! We burst out of the atmosphere into the blackness.

But the rattling didn't stop, in fact it got worse. The rocket was shaking so much it felt like it was going to tip over.

"Hey, what's going on?" Fernando jabbed at the control desk. "It's not working!"

Everyone started screaming and the shutter by my seat popped open. Outside, even though the room was juddering up and down, I spotted Darius and Spike dancing about on the platform below and waving Darius's phone in the air.

CREAK! SNAP! WRENCH!

"The launch pad...it's breaking. We're going to be blasted into space...for real!" howled Fernando.

Everyone screamed even louder.

"Hey, big guy, we need to do something!" Chip yelled, thumping me in the leg with one of his potato sides.

"Do we?"

"Yes... it's up to you, Spudboy."

"Is it?"

"YEEEES!"

My tummy twitched. My skin tingled. I felt hot and itchy.

My heart was hammering at a hundred miles an hour.

I didn't know what to do.

"Oh...oh..."

"COME ON," Chip shouted.

I felt a hair sprout out of my shoulder.

Something was happening to me.

Something strange. I unclipped my seat belt.

"Where are you going?" Alfie whimpered,

his face as white as toothpaste.

"To save us," I said without thinking,

although I had no idea what I was going to do.

My seat was in the middle of the rocket,

which meant that it was about four metres off

the ground.

I looked over the side, and blinked. The

only way was down.

So that's the way I went. Swinging my leg

over the arm of my seat, I gave Alfie a pat on

the shoulder and lowered myself over the edge. My arms felt as strong as rope as I climbed down past each seat. The only time I'd tried to climb a ladder before I'd got stuck halfway up but this felt easy.

Everyone was in such a panic they didn't seem to notice as I climbed past.

I landed at the bottom of the rocket and glanced at my hands. My skin was bubbling like foam in a bath. Sweat poured down my face and something was rising inside me like a giant wave.

I fell to the floor and crawled behind Ms Brimstone's seat at the bottom of the rocket.

Hugging my knees in close, I curled into a ball and shut my eyes. The giant wave inside me smashed and crashed, I felt like a tiny boat being thrown onto the rocks.

"AAAAAAAAAARGH!"

A roar came from somewhere very close to me. I opened my eyes. The roar was coming out of *my* mouth.

As I jumped up the rocket shuddered.

"Do something Fernando," Ms Brimstone demanded.

"I can't stop it!" Fernando yelled. "This has never happened before. It's like someone else is driving. We're out of control."

"AHHHHHHHHHHHHHH," everyone went

crazy.

"OK, Spudboy, there's no time to lose. We

need to get the rocket door open," said Chip

from the floor. He must've fallen out of my

pocket when I was curled into a ball.

I grabbed the door lock and pulled but it

wouldn't budge. We were sealed in for take-off!

I rammed the door with my shoulder,

which really hurt. The door didn't seem to

notice. Chip bounced onto my shoulder and

whispered.

"Focus, Spudboy, you can do this. Use

your Potato Power."

I looked at Chip. His scratchy, denty face seemed serious.

I took two steps back and crouched into a start position, like a sprinter. Closing my eyes, I breathed in and held my breath. Inside, wave after wave of energy shot from my feet to the top of my head, before smashing into a million potatoey pieces in my brain. With a fiery blast of the engines, the rocket lifted off the platform and into the air, before stopping suddenly. Something was holding it to the earth.

I waited for the next wave to come. It rose from my feet, past my knees and into my tummy, then it started to surge up to my head, and I ran...

"Raaaaaaaargh!"

Bang! Crunch! Clatter!

The rocket door flew off its hinges and clanked down onto the platform.

"Phew."

"Awesome, Spudboy! That's one mangled rocket door. Now let's get everyone out of here."

"Chip, where are my glasses? I can't see anything."

"Use your eyes."

"What? But I can't see without my glasses."

"Your *other* eyes," Chip called from the rocket floor.

"Huh?"

"Potatoes have eyes all over the place, Spudboy. You just gotta learn to use them."

As Chip spoke, my head started to ache like someone was spinning my brain around or swapping it for a jacket potato. Another wave of potato power flowed through me and my tummy flipped. I was going to be sick *again*! I rolled to the open rocket door and stuck my head outside, gulping down fresh air. The room whirled about my head like a kaleidoscope then, as if someone had flicked a switch, it all became clear and I could see everything.

Not like I normally see things with my glasses on. Now I could see *everything* in the room, even the things that were behind me, or to the side. Without looking up, I knew what was happening on the ceiling! I had an eye in the top of my head.

The rocket engines fired again and the wires holding them to the platform strained.

"They're going to snap," I shouted. My potato vision picked up a movement on the other side of the room.

Spike was holding Darius's phone like a remote control, aiming it at the rocket. He stabbed the screen with his finger. As the rocket strained on the wires, Spike began punching the screen desperately. Darius covered his eyes.

Ting ting ting! The wires snapped like three kite strings being cut.

# Chapter 11

# Mash Slide

Boom!

Air rushed past the doorway, sending me flying back into the bottom of the rocket, as we blasted towards the glass ceiling.

SMASH!

Pieces of glass rained in and bounced off my back and shoulders. I didn't feel a thing. My new, thick potatoey skin was protecting me like armour.

"Ahhhh, I want my muuuuum," screamed Tabitha.

"I want mine!" squealed Fernando.

As another wave of potato power raced up my body, I swivelled round and down onto one knee. I had no idea what I was about to do. We were heading up into the sky, and there was no door on the rocket!

"Use your power," Chip said, "this rocket's about to go into orbit and, as far as I can tell, no one here is a trained astronaut."

With the ground getting further away, I aimed the palms of my hands out of the door hole and focussed all my potato eyes on the platform below. Concentrating as hard as I could, I sent a bolt of energy down each arm.

Streams of extra-thick, triple-strength mega

mash shot out of my hands all the way down

through the smashed ceiling. I turned my hands

left and right, wrapping the two streams of high

powered potato goo around the platform. Then,

just like I was doing up a pair of giant gungy

shoelaces, I tied the streams together in a

double knot.

And the rocket jolted to a stop, a

hundred metres above the Science Museum.

"Wow, I never knew I could do that!"

"Us spuds are full of surprises, kid," said

Chip, from the floor.

There was a moment of silence; everyone was too frightened to speak.

Down below, the Science Museum looked a like a mini model of a Science Museum, surrounded by roads full of toy cars and buses. The people walking along the pavements were just little moving dots. This couldn't be our last view of the Earth, could it? I had to act fast.

"What happened?" asked Ms Brimstone.

"We've stopped." cried Fernando from his seat at the front. "We're saved!"

"We're not safe yet, Fernando, are we?" growled Ms Brimstone, "Children – do not undo your seatbelts. Stay exactly where you are. I'm sure I can find a way to get us back down."

No one had noticed what I'd been up to at the bottom of the space craft. I knew the mega mash wouldn't hold the rocket forever.

"We need to evacuate," I called up the aisle, attaching the mega mash shoelaces securely to the side of the rocket with a fresh blob of extra-gloopy potato.

Ms Brimstone turned round in her seat and looked at me.

"Oh!" she gasped, "Who...or what...are you?"

All the children looked back down the aisle.

"Oh my...

"Who's that?"

"Is it a potato?"

No one seemed to recognise me.

"Where's Colin?" sobbed Alfie.

"He must have fallen out," Eddie Zedder said.

"Colin's fallen out!"

"Colin Sludge fell out of the rocket."

"Sludge is dead!"

The whispers went round and round.

"No, I'm..." I started to say, but Chip nudged my ankle.

"Let's get everyone outta here," he said.

I nodded, picked up Chip and put him in my pocket.

"Follow me everyone!"

The mega mash had started to go solid like a massive slide, so I dived head first through the door way onto it. In a second, I'd zoomed back down to Earth and in through the hole in the museum roof.

It was time to tackle Spike and Darius.

As soon as I popped out of the end of the potato slide onto the platform, I saw them rushing towards the exit.

"We have to stop them. We have to get that mobile phone!" I said to Chip. "It's the only way to bring the rocket back to earth."

I fired a blob of mash out of my hand which splatted perfectly onto the exit door handle, jamming it shut. There was no way they'd be able to open that.

As Alfie and Sarah shot off the potato slide behind me, in one swift movement, I forward rolled off the platform and onto the floor. Then, I rolled after Spike and Darius. Chip was right; rolling really was the fastest way for a potato to move.

In an instant, I'd reached the exit where Spike was trying to prise the mash lock open.

"I can't do it, Darius...we're going to get in so much trouble because of your stupid phone."

"Don't move and put your hands up," was all I could think of to say.

Spike span round and looked at me, his face shiny with sweat.

"Yuurgh! Darius...it's a...a...monster."

Darius lifted his eyes from the controls of his phone.

"I have no idea what *that* is," he said, calmly.

He aimed the phone at my head.

"This contains a laser, which will fry you in a nanosecond."

# Chapter 12

## Chip Finger

I put my hands up. Even my potato skin was no match for a laser.

"Let's get him, Spike," Darius said, grinning.

Spike lunged at me and shoved me hard in the chest.

"You freak. What are you…a parsnip?" he snarled.

Back on the other side of the room, more and more children from the class were zipping off the end of the potato slide and standing on

the damaged platform confused.

My mash wouldn't hold the rocket

forever. I had to get that phone and switch it

off...somehow.

Spike shoved me again. Without him

noticing, I slipped my hand into my pocket and

pulled out Chip.

"Do something Chip," I whispered, as I

dropped my potato pal to the floor hoping no

one would spot him.

Chip started rolling towards Darius, but

he didn't get far.

"Hey, what's that?" yelped Spike.

"It's a potato, obviously," Darius said, taking aim with his laser phone. "Target practice."

With a fixed grin, Darius pressed the button on his phone and a beam of red light cut across the room.

"No!" I yelled, throwing myself onto the ground over Chip.

Nothing happened.

I rolled over. A dot of red light was moving in circles on my chest and Darius was smirking at Spike.

"That scared you, Mr Parsnip Freak, didn't it? Thought your pet potato was about to be roast. It's just a light."

The biggest wave of energy ever rumbled up through my body and out of my mouth.

"Raaaargh!" I roared, pointing my index finger at the phone in Darius's hand.

ZZZZZZPPPPPPP

A single, golden chip fired out of my finger like an arrow.

Crack. A direct hit.

The phone span into the air and clattered onto floor. Its screen cracked and the battery fell out of the back. I dived onto the pieces and scooped them up.

"Oh dear, now the controls really *are* broken, aren't they?" snarled Darius.

There was a huge cheer behind me, as Fernando and Ms Brimstone flopped off the potato slide into a crowd of waiting children. And just in time, as the mega mash slide started to soften and crumple.

"My rocket, my rocket, it's gone for ever!" wailed Fernando, looking up through the hole in the roof. He fell to his knees and sobbed so much his whole body vibrated right to the tips of his zig-zaggy hair.

Ms Brimstone tapped him on the shoulder.

"Excuse me, Fernando, but your rocket seems to be fine. Look."

She pointed through the broken glass ceiling. The soft mash slide was folding back towards us, lowering the rocket gently down to earth. Smashing the phone must've switched off the rocket's engines.

I looked over at Darius, and gave him a little wink. I couldn't help myself.

He snorted and shook his head.

"Take out the batteries and you override the system. Well done, Mr Parsnip Freak. Sometimes the simplest solution is the hardest to see, isn't it Spike?"

"I don't know," said Spike scuffing the floor with his feet, "you said there was no way to stop it."

The rocket simulator gently came in to land on the platform, sitting on a bed of fluffy mash like a giant sausage.

"That was so cooooool!" said Alfie Radish, unclipping his visor and beaming inside his space helmet, "a real live launch. This has been the best school trip EVER."

Whack!

The mash lock I'd put on the door split in half, the door opened and five Science Museum security guards piled into the room. Spike and Darius were cornered. Darius glared at me coldly and Spike hung his head as they were led over to Ms Brimstone. While the guards were checking that everyone was OK, me and Chip snuck into the boys' toilet.

"Well, I guess that's the last we'll hear from Darius and Spike for a while," I said, putting Chip down next to the sink.

"I wouldn't bet on it," said Chip, "They'll be up to their tricks again before too long."

"What is *that?*"

I was looking in the mirror. The creature looking back at me was the strangest thing I'd ever seen. His skin was hard and yellow. All over his face and arms were dents, scuffs and scratches. Long hairs, as thick as straw, stuck up out of his shoulders through his shirt. And he had no glasses on.

"That's you, Spudboy," Chip said quietly.

I stared and stared and stared. I didn't blink once as I watched myself slowly transform back to Colin Sludge.

Back out in the rocket room, the Security Guards were questioning everyone about what happened. Spike and Darius were standing next to Ms Brimstone, who looked angrier than I'd ever seen her before.

"But...but...we only meant to make the simulator better!" complained Spike.

"Not another word from you," snapped Ms Brimstone, "thanks to you we owe the

Science Museum a new rocket. You two boys will be on detention for the rest of your lives!"

Alfie Radish trotted over to me, his space helmet under his arm like an astronaut.

"Colin, where've you been? I thought you were...dead."

"No, I was in the toilet. I must've gone just before the rocket took off," I said.

Alfie reached into his pocket.

"I found your glasses," he said, handing me my specs.

"Thanks Alfie."

"That's OK. You missed an amazing trip,

there was this incredible slide that tasted like

mashed potato!"

# Chapter 13

## Roll on Home Time

"Thanks for the lift, big guy, it sure beats rolling."

"That's OK, Chip," I said, holding the potato up on the palm of my hand as we walked home.

"We did a great job today, Spudboy. What a team," Chip said, turning around on my hand and looking at me. The lines on his potato face stretched into a wide smile.

"So I really didn't imagine any of this, Chip?"

"*Imagine it?* Spudboy, take it from me, you're unique. You have powers like no one else...except me, but I'm more of a potato than a person. Together, we're unstoppable."

I stopped walking, held Chip up in front of my face and looked at him closely.

"I guess we are," I said, and a warm feeling spread through my body, or at least my left leg...

It was Milton! He was weeing on me!

"Get off!"

"Milton, stop that you pesky piddler!"

Mrs Sticklebee prodded Milton with her walking stick and the tiddly dog scampered off to find a lamppost.

"Are you OK, Colin?"

"Yes, don't worry, I'll just have to wash my trousers."

"Your trousers will be fine. However, this morning you were talking to your school bag and now you're talking to a potato." Mrs Sticklebee smiled, and waited for an explanation.

"Oh. Yes. Well, it's a school project...to find out what the friendliest vegetable is."

She smiled more, showing the gap between her teeth, and shook her head.

"A carrot is the friendliest vegetable, Colin," she said, with a wink. "Come on Milton; let's get you home."

"That is one crazy lady," Chip said, once Mrs Sticklebee had gone. "Most of the carrots I know have serious issues."

When I got home, Mum and Dad were watching TV.

"It's incredible, Terry," Mum said.

"It certainly is," replied Dad.

"What *is* that thing?"

"I don't know, Sue, but it *looks* like

a...like a...an enormous walking potato. Must be

a costume of some sort."

I sat down on the sofa next to Dad.

"Hey look at this, Colin, a giant potato.

This could be really good for business, don't

you think? The public profile of potatoes will be

sky high!"

The news was on. They had CCTV footage

from the Science Museum. Apparently, there'd

been an accident with one of the flight

simulators and some kind of strange super hero

had turned up to save the day before

disappearing without a word.

Who'd've thought it?

"The costume is amazing, so realistic,"

Dad said, leaning right up close to the TV. "I

can't think of a better disguise than a potato.

Hey Susan, if we could work out who it is, he

could be Mama Sludge's mascot! We could

sponsor him like those companies who get their

names on football shirts. Imagine that – we'd be

world famous too.  Good idea, eh, Colin?"

"Erm...yeah...." I said, feeling Chip

chuckling in my pocket.

"Well, it's a lovely idea, Terry but how are

we ever going to get in touch with him? No one

has a clue who he is. We'll just have to keep

trying the new recipes and hope he turns up for

tea!"

Mum looked at me and smiled.

"Right, My Little Peeler, we can't sit here

watching TV all night can we?" she said, getting

up from the sofa, "We've got a batch of Mint

Chocolate Chip mash to make and there's a big

bag of spuds in the kitchen with your name on

it."

And for the first time in a long time, I

thought that might not be such a bad thing.

## About the Author – David Windle

Thanks for reading Spudboy and Chip – I really hope you enjoyed the first book in the series! I work as a primary school teacher in South London and you can contact me via www.primarypoems.com.

Printed in Great Britain
by Amazon